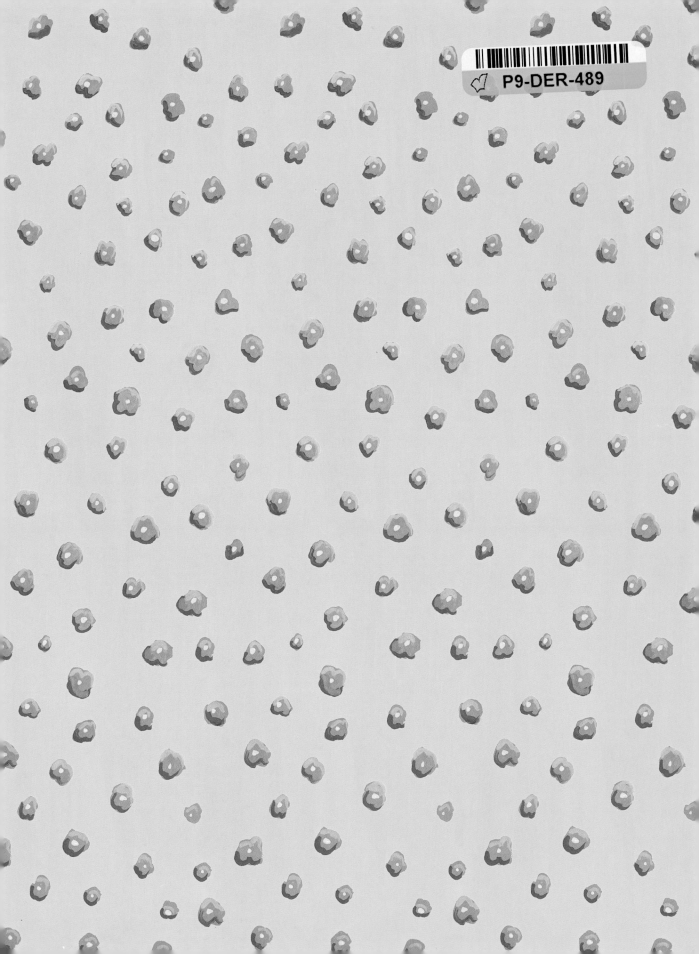

Elinor and Violet

THE STORY OF TWO NAUGHTY CHICKENS

by Patti Beling Murphy

Little, Brown and Company
Boston   New York   London

For Camille Rose, my own Elinor

First Edition

Library of Congress Cataloging-in-Publication Data
Murphy, Patti Beling.
  Elinor and Violet / written and illustrated by Patti Beling Murphy. — 1st ed.
   p.   cm.
  Summary: When Elinor, who is sometimes just a little naughty, makes friends
with Violet, who is much naughtier, Elinor almost spoils the visit of her
favorite aunt.
  ISBN 0-316-91088-0
  [Behavior—Fiction.] I. Title.
PZ7.M9547El 2000
[E]—dc21   99-27485

10 9 8 7 6 5 4 3 2 1

TWP

Printed in Singapore

The paintings for this book were done in gouache on watercolor paper.
The text was set in Bernhard Gothic, and the display type is Providence Sans.

Elinor was just a little bit naughty.

She wrote on the walls — but in tiny, tiny letters where no one could see it. She took her sisters' things and hid them in her room — but only their not-so-special things.

She talked back to her mother — but not out loud.
Sometimes, she sang bad words softly under her breath in the
bathroom. Although she tried to be good some of the time,
she kind of liked being naughty.

One day, Elinor took her babies for a walk and met a little
girl who had come to stay with her grandmother.

Her name was Violet and she was *very* naughty.

She wrote on the walls with her special indelible markers.

She talked back to *everyone*.

She sang bad words very loudly while walking down the street.

"She's even naughtier than Elinor," said Elinor's sisters. "We don't like her!"

"I do," said Elinor.

Violet and Elinor played together every day that week.

They thought of many naughty things to do...

. . . like leaving the water running in the bathtub to see how
long it would take to run out under the door.

"You don't have to go when your mother calls you," Violet said. "Just don't answer."

Elinor was impressed. She tried it.

Elinor spent more and more time in the time-out corner.

On Saturday, Violet's last day at her grandmother's house, Elinor's Aunt Lucy came to visit on her way home from her trip around the world. She was everyone's favorite, especially Elinor's. Aunt Lucy wore fabulous clothes. And she always took Elinor and her sisters out to tea and let them eat all the sandwiches and

cakes they wanted.

"Are we going out to tea?" Elinor asked. "Can my new friend Violet come with us? Please, please, please?"

"Yes, but we won't be going out for at least an hour." With that, Aunt Lucy disappeared into the kitchen to chat with Elinor's mother.

"How about we pretend we're evil pirates and bury lots of treasure?" Violet said. "And we'll pinkie-swear not to tell where it is!"

"Yes, yes!" Elinor replied.

They gathered up pieces of treasure and hid them in nooks and crannies all over the house.

"Now we just need one more *special* treasure," said Violet, eyeing Aunt Lucy's purse.

"Oh, no, I don't think that's such a good idea," said Elinor. "That belongs to Aunt Lucy and we shouldn't touch it."

"Pooh pooh," said Violet, gathering up the purse.

Elinor followed her quietly up the stairs.

After hiding the treasure, the girls sang sea chanteys and made Elinor's sisters' dolls walk the plank. As the very last doll fell screaming into the ocean, they heard closet doors opening and shutting, and Aunt Lucy sighing.

After much banging and crashing, Aunt Lucy appeared in
the doorway.

"Has anyone seen my purse?" she asked. "We can't go out
to tea until we find it. My car keys and money are in it."

"No," said Elinor, not daring to look up.

"Are you sure?" Aunt Lucy said. "It's filled with presents from my trip."

Elinor looked at Violet. Violet wiggled her pinkie at Elinor and whispered, "Pinkie-swear!"

Elinor's sisters scowled at them and at their dolls scattered all over the floor. "Now you've done it, Elinor," they said. "Now we can't go out to tea."

Elinor did not know what to do. She looked from Aunt Lucy to Violet. She looked up and she looked down. Then she knew.

"It's buried treasure," Elinor squeaked. "We'll find it, we'll find it!" she promised, and dragged Violet upstairs to look.

When the girls brought the purse downstairs, Elinor's mother, Aunt Lucy, and Elinor's sisters were all waiting.

Elinor just looked at Aunt Lucy and began to sob.

"I'm sorry, Aunt Lucy," she said.

"Me too," said Violet.

"Oh, Elinor," Aunt Lucy said, "everyone's naughty sometimes. Once, your mom and I put salt in the sugar bowl when
our piano teacher was coming to visit. Now let's go out to tea!"

They all had a marvelous time eating little cakes with pink frosting and tiny spun-sugar roses.

Elinor was careful to sit up very straight, and to say please and thank you, and was only a little naughty at the very end,

when she slipped some sugar cubes into her pocket.

Violet only blew bubbles in her tea once and did not take
even one sugar cube.

Later that day, Violet walked over to Elinor's house to say good-bye. She gave Elinor one of her special indelible markers and her address.

"Guess what!" said Violet. "Next year, I'll be at Grandma's for the whole summer!"

Elinor hugged Violet good-bye and secretly slipped a sugar cube into her pocket.

"Phew," said Elinor's mother as she tucked her into bed that night. "I must say I'm glad that's over."

Elinor just smiled.

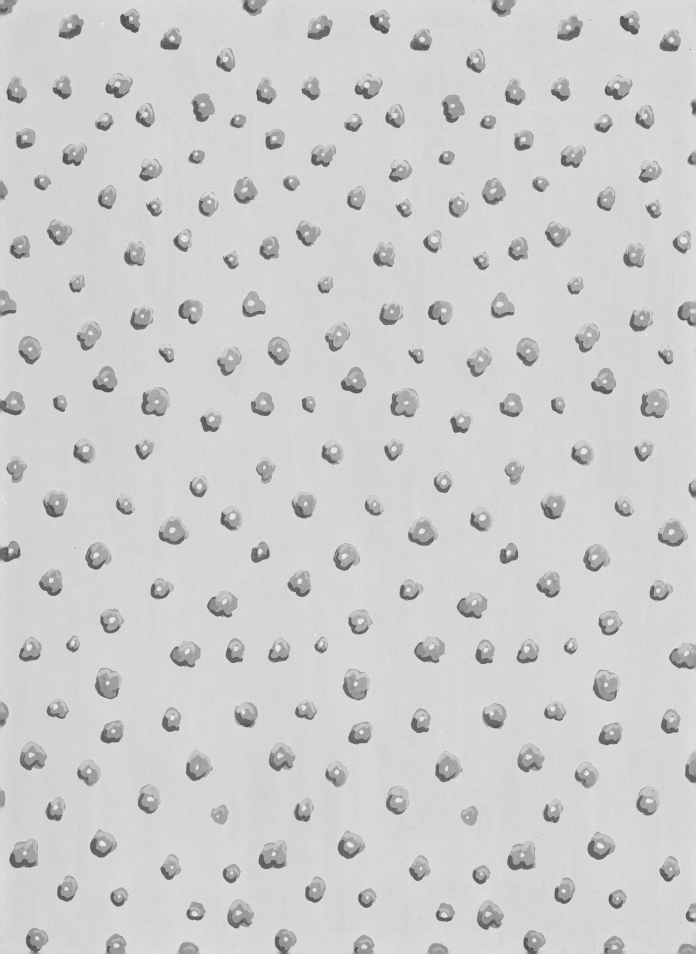